THE DOCTORS
THE ARCHIVE

HAPPY TIMES AND PLACES

Saturday, November 23, 2013 marks the golden jubilee of a very British phenomenon.

It will be exactly 50 years to the day since a policeman approached an old junkyard in Totter's Lane in London, and found a police box inside, humming with energy. This was the very first episode of the series, An Unearthly Child.

Since then, the Doctor has gone on to change his face many times, from William Hartnell to Patrick Troughton, from Jon Pertwee to Tom Baker, from Peter Davison to Colin Baker, Sylvester McCoy into Paul McGann, then Christopher Eccleston into David Tennant and Matt Smith, who in turn will regenerate into the 12th Doctor, Peter Capaldi, on Christmas Day this year.

Over the years, the Doctor has had many friends by his side – Susan, Ian, Barbara, Steven, Jamie, Zoe, Leela, Adric, Peri, Ace, Rose, Jack, Amy and Clara, to name but a few.

But he's also had a silent companion at his side all the way too, chronicling his adventures virtually from day one – the Daily Mirror. We've been there at press calls over the years, capturing forever those behind-the-scenes moments that would now be recorded as DVD extras. And we've even been with the Doctor on screen. When his companion Ace wants to know the football scores in 1988's silver anniversary story, Silver Nemesis, she picks up the Mirror to see how Charlton Athletic have done!

We've an amazing wealth of images from every era of the show, from its earliest days up to the present, collected together here for the first time.

CONTENTS

A Mirror publication
Head of Syndication & Licensing: Fergus McKenna
Mirrorpix: David Scripps
020 7293 3858

Produced by Trinity Mirror Media
PO BOX 48, Liverpool L69 3EB
ISBN 9781907 324321

Managing Director: Ken Rogers
Publishing Director: Steve Hanrahan
Executive Art Editor: Rick Cooke
Senior Editor: Paul Dove
Words by: Kenny Smith
Designed and produced by: Roy Gilfoyle and Adam Oldfield

Part of the Mirror Collection
Images: Mirrorpix
Printed by William Gibbons

MYTH MAKERS

November 1963 sees the birth of a British television legend

In the 21st century, the BBC was struggling to win the ratings war with ITV on Saturday nights.

So, when looking to the future, they looked to the past for their new strategy. And at the heart of it was Doctor Who.

For years, Doctor Who was unloved, a show which had been allowed to stumble on with no love from BBC management, before the series was finally axed in 1989.

But in the 1960s, Doctor Who was conceived with a deliberate role to fill – to plug the gap between the football pools on Grandstand, and the show that got the younger people watching, Juke Box Jury. It led to the creation of family viewing, with a schedule that would keep viewers hooked to the one channel, without feeling the temptation to turn over to the other side (in the days of just two television channels).

Doctor Who was conceived by Sydney Newman, a Canadian TV producer whom the BBC were able to poach to take over their drama department.

Over the period of several months, a clever and carefully-selected team developed Newman's idea of an elderly time traveller taking humans into the past, and into the future, in a series he envisaged as being educational for children.

His key appointment was the young and brilliant Verity Lambert as producer, having worked with Newman at Thames. She very quickly assembled a brilliant cast, who brought the characters of the Doctor, his granddaughter Susan, and school teachers Ian Chesterton and Barbara Wright to life.

The part of the leading man went to William Hartnell, a star of stage and screen for many years, who had never particularly been seen in 'good guy' roles. Carole Ann Ford was cast as Susan, and Jacqueline Hill was given the role of Barbara. William Russell – a familiar face on TV thanks to his starring role as Sir Lancelot on ITV in the 1950s – took the role of Chesterton.

Months of work behind the scenes were finally realised on November 23, 1963, when the first episode of Doctor Who aired, and two school teachers discovered nothing at the end of the lane, apart from an old police box in a junkyard.

British television history was about to be made...

TRAILBLAZERS: (left) The First Doctor William Hartnell is visited by fan Steven Qualtrough at the BBC in 1964, (top) Doctor Who creator Sydney Newman, (middle) the series' first producer Verity Lambert and (above) the Doctor's first companion Carole Ann Ford

THE DALEKS

When Raymond Cusick designed the Daleks in 1963, little did he know he was creating a design icon of the 20th century.

And amazingly, Raymond received only £80 for designing the legendary aliens – because he was a simple BBC staff member. Terry Nation, the writer who dreamed up the creatures, went on to earn millions.

Sadly, Raymond died in February 2013 after a short illness, at the age of 84.

In a 2005 exclusive interview with the Daily Mirror, Raymond said: "I was told 'You do realise Raymond that there are people who would give their right arm to work for the BBC – you're lucky to have a job'.

"I came to terms with the fact that I was employed by the BBC, but that really upset me and it was one of the reasons I left."

Royalty payments worth tens of thousands of pounds still go to the estate of Terry Nation, who wrote the original Dalek script, and BBC funds.

The Daleks were so popular after their initial appearance in 1963 that they became a regular opponent for the Doctor in the early years, facing William Hartnell in four stories in just over two years.

But Raymond eventually quit the series in 1966, in disgust at getting little credit for his iconic design.

"I worked on the programme for three years but quite honestly, I got fed up with it.

"Nobody, apart from my bosses, was actually saying thanks to me.

"The producer Verity Lambert and the Head of

Raymond Cusick on how he designed some iconic villains on a shoestring budget – and how he fell out of love with the BBC

Design at the time Richard Levin were a bit upset about it. They got me an ex-gratia payment of £100, which after income tax, came to £80, 10 shillings and sixpence.

"When you are a BBC employee, you sign a 14-page contract and all my work over the years belonged to the BBC."

And Raymond, who went on to design hundreds of shows as a BBC staff designer until he retired in 1988, felt disillusioned when so many people in showbiz tried to claim credit for his Dalek vision.

"I eventually got a letter from the BBC's Head of Programmes saying 'Thank you very much'. But there were all sorts of extraneous people trying to muscle in," he said.

"I got fed up and thought 'To hell with it' and I asked to be taken off the series. Lo and behold, I was given some single TV plays to do – and they were all about science fiction!"

A common myth is that the Dalek design was based on pepper-pots, said Raymond.

He explains "the truth" is that he threw ideas about with Bill Roberts, from Shawcraft Models in Uxbridge, Middlesex, a company that made the costumes.

"We went to lunch in the canteen and I was scribbling on the back of napkins the ideas of the Daleks. I picked up what could have been a saltpot and moved it around the table top," said Raymond.

"I said 'It moves like that - without any limbs or legs'. The design was already partly on paper and partly in my head at the time."

Amazingly, Raymond was only given the job because then design colleague Ridley Scott – the future Hollywood director – wasn't available.

The first four Daleks, made from fibre glass, were built on a total budget of £250. "Miniscule," he adds.

Although he doesn't receive a penny more for the iconic look he designed, Raymond was still touched when fans showed their appreciation.

"I was doing a question and answer at a fan convention in Liverpool and they all stood up and gave me a standing ovation. I couldn't believe it. I won't forget that."

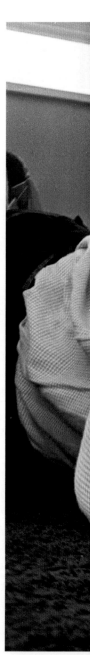

ICONIC FIGURES:
(left) Terry Nation – the man who dreamed up the idea of Daleks (second and third left) More pictures of Raymond Cusick with his family and a miniature Dalek

FAMILY AFFAIR:
Raymond Cusick with his daughter and a model of a Dalek in 1965

"I was scribbling on the back of napkins the ideas of the Daleks. I picked up what could have been a saltpot and moved it around the table"

RUBBERNECKING:
Carole Ann Ford
is carried off by
a Voord, an outer
space creature
with webbed
hands and feet

THE KEYS OF MARINUS

Doctor and companions tackle flipper-footed foe as alien race battles for control of super-computer

Doctor Who had struck gold with its first alien creatures.

The Daleks were an overnight success, and when the TARDIS next landed on an alien world, Terry Nation was once again the writer.

The Keys of Marinus saw the Doctor and his companions arrive on an island, in the middle of a sea of acid. There, they met Arbitan, an inhabitant of planet Marinus, where the populace could be pacified by inserting micro-circuits into a super-computer.

Unfortunately for the people of Marinus, a dissenting people were standing up to its rulers, intent on causing trouble and taking control of Marinus. Yartek, leader of the alien Voord, was determind to control the keys.

The Doctor and his friends were able to save the day by ensuring that Yartek failed to take control of the super-computer.

Yartek, though, wasn't helped by the fact that his people wore a totally impractical costume. The Voord were encased from head to foot in rubber outfits, with distinctive angled masks at the top, and on the bottom... flippers.

Unfortunately, . during episode six of the story, one of the Voord very visibly trips over its own flipper, and in the days when a retake would have been very costly, remained in the finished programme.

The Voord were the first of many alien species to try to steal the Daleks' crown as Doctor Who's top rivals. And they failed – the Voord were never seen again on TV

The Dalek Invasion of Earth

With the Doctor and his friends having visited the Daleks in their homeworld, it seemed only polite that the alien creatures should visit Earth.

The Dalek Invasion of Earth was the second story of Doctor Who's second season, giving the Daleks a chance to prove they weren't one-hit wonders.

Terry Nation was once again the writer, setting the action in a devastated London in the year 2167. The Daleks had invaded years earlier, enslaving humanity, by conquering and destroying those who stood against them.

But the Daleks weren't invading for no apparent reason – they were mining the magnetic core of the Earth, removing it so they could replace it with a motor, to pilot the planet anywhere they chose. The mine was based in Bedfordshire.

The story – highlighting the return of the Daleks – was given the front cover of the Radio Times to publicise it, and the first episode featured the memorable image of the Doctor and Ian Chesterton trying to escape from a group of the Daleks' slaves, Robomen, by swimming in the Thames – only to

As the evil enemy strike London, the Go Go's craft a musical tribute

see a Dalek emerge from the waves.

Broadcast from November to December 1964, the story was also notable for the departure of Carole Ann Ford from the programme, who felt that the character of Susan hadn't developed in the way she had hoped.

And while the Daleks invaded the fictional London in the future, as the programme was being transmitted, another Dalek invasion took place in the present day.

The Daleks came to Bond Street in London, where a new pop group, calling themselves the Go Go's borrowed the BBC's props, which were appearing on TV at the time, and took them to London's West End shortly before recording their song, I'm Gonna Spent My Christmas With A Dalek on November 25, 1964.

The Go Go's were Mike Johnson (19), Alan Cairns

CAPITAL CHAOS: The Daleks frighten people in the centre of London, while Verity Lambert poses with one

(20), Abe Harris (20), Bill Davison (22), Les McLeian (19) and Sue Smith (17).

The song, however, failed to get a grasp on the most evil and vicious race in the universe:

"I'm gonna spend my Christmas with a Dalek,
"And hug him under the mistletoe,
"And if he's very nice,
"I'll feed him sugar spice,
"And hang a Christmas stocking from his big left toe.
"And when we both get up on Christmas morning
"I'll kiss him on his chromium-plated head
"And take him in to say hi to Mum
"And frighten daddy out of his bed!"

The song, which wasn't authorised by the BBC or Terry Nation, featured the Dalek (which didn't sound like a Dalek) wishing the listener a Merry Christmas, as well as stating: "I wish to be your friend," and also asked, "Please may I have some more plum pud-ding and cus-tard?"

The Go Go's are not known to have recorded a second single.

BIG HIT:
The Go Go's pose with the Daleks on the streets of London in November 1964

The Rescue

Doctor travels to the planet Dido to free crash survivor from the grasp of the evil Koquillion

I WILL GO DOWN WITH THIS SHIP: Vicki, played by Maureen O'Brien gets to grips with Koquillion after her spaceship crash-lands on the planet Dido

Over the years, Doctor Who has seen many changes to its line-up.

Doctors and their companions have regularly come and gone since Carole Ann Ford became the first of the show's cast to depart the TARDIS.

When the Doctor left his granddaughter on an Earth devastated by the Dalek Invasion of Earth in 2167, his travels next took him to the planet Dido.

There he met the orphaned Vicki, the only survivor of a spaceship crash, who was being menaced by the evil Koquillion.

Vicki was played by Maureen O'Brien, who was later unit general manager Elizabeth Straker in the second season of Casualty in 1987, and also appeared in other programmes including Taggart, Cracker, A Touch of Frost and Heartbeat.

In recent years, Maureen has become a successful crime novelist, featuring Detective Inspector John Bright.

THE FIRST DOCTOR

Hartnell makes leaps through time with a mature makeover

ART TO HART:
Make-up artist Sonia Markham applies the finishing touches to William Hartnell's wig in 1966

William Hartnell was aged just 55 when he was cast as the First Doctor – but to viewers he seemed far older.

Indeed, actor David Bradley, who portrayed Hartnell in a special drama covering the origins of Doctor Who as part of the golden anniversary celebrations, looks roughly the same age as Hartnell – and Bradley was 70 at the time of recording!

To help give Hartnell his extra years, part of his weekly make-up routine was to fit him with a wig at the BBC studios.

The Mirror is proud to present these pictures showing make-up artist Sonia Markham applying the finishing touches to his face make-up and wig, at BBC Television Centre on January 9 1966, just days before the transmission of the show's 100th episode, Escape Switch, episode 10 of The Daleks' Master Plan.

THE WEB PLANET

From venom grubs to the Zarbi, Vortis provides all manner of alien creatures for the Time Lord and his team to conquer

Over the years, the Doctor has encountered many weird and wonderful creatures.

From the crab-like Macra to the rhino-headed Judoon, from the Fish People of Atlantis to the Cheetah people of a dying alien world, the Time Lord has met many odd aliens.

But none are as strange as those encountered on the planet Vortis, in 1965's The Web Planet.

It was the first Doctor Who story in which the regular cast of the Doctor, Ian Chesterton, Barbara Wright and Vicki were the only people with a human appearance.

They met giant ants known as the Zarbi, the butterfly-like Menoptera, the insectoid Optera, the caterpillar-esque venom grubs and the spidery Carsenome.

For six weeks, the Doctor and his friends fought against the Zarbi, venom grubs and Carsenome, before finally defeating their foes.

ROBOT WARS: The Daleks and the Mechonoids come face to face in The Chase

THE CHASE

Daleks v Mechonoids – but there could only be one winner

Dalekmania was at its height in 1965, as the public couldn't get enough of the evil creatures.

Dalek dress-up costumes, soap, water pistols (sold as anti-Dalek fluid neutralisers), slippers, toys and novelty records invaded British stores, in a way the Daleks themselves never could without being foiled by the Doctor.

To satisfy the public's appetite for Daleks, they returned for a third story, The Chase, which saw the departures of William Russell and Jacqueline Hill from the series.

But with every departure from the TARDIS, there is an arrival, and joining the crew was future Blue Peter legend Peter Purves, as space pilot Steven Taylor.

Peter recalled: "My first story was with the Daleks in The Chase. I played an American tourist called Morton Dill, who takes the mickey

out of them in one of the early episodes, and I think I was the only person who ever got to do that.

"Then I was asked to come back a few weeks later and got the part of Steven Taylor.

"I never liked working with the Daleks. They trundled around in rehearsals with the top half off, and you would have the voice coming from off-set. They were never the easiest things to act with."

The Chase saw the Daleks face off against another robotic race, the Mechonoids, created by Terry Nation in the hope they would rival his original monsters.

Despite being brought to life by Raymond Cusick, who had designed the Daleks, the Mechonoids never captured the public's imagination in the same way the Daleks did, and they were never seen again on screen.

APPEARANCES CAN BE DECEPTIVE: The Drahvins from the planet Drahva weren't as nice as they looked

Galaxy 4

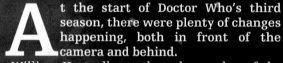

A t the start of Doctor Who's third season, there were plenty of changes happening, both in front of the camera and behind.

William Hartnell was the only member of the original cast who was left, and producer Verity Lambert was departing for pastures new having established her credentials within the BBC.

The first story of season three, Galaxy 4, saw the Doctor, Vicki and new companion Steven – played by Peter Purves – land on a planet which was on the verge of destruction.

There, they were encountered by beautiful Drahvins, and the monstrous Rills, but the Doctor and his friends soon discovered that appearances were deceptive, as the Rills were friendly, unlike the Drahvins.

After the original episodes were shown, the BBC made film copies for overseas sales, but as television moved into the colour era, the original videotapes and film copies were destroyed.

However, in 2011, a copy of episode three of Galaxy 4 was recovered by the BBC from a private collector.

Peter Purves said: "It was an interesting one to watch, as I'd never seen it before. I never watched them when they went out. All I ever saw was what was on the monitors when we recorded them.

"I don't remember too much about it, or the details of the story, although years later I recorded narration for the release of the surviving soundtrack, which was interesting."

The Daleks' Master Plan

I n the 21st century, the Christmas Day episode of Doctor Who is regarded as a highlight of the festive season TV schedule.

But the idea of a Christmas episode of the show is nothing new, as it had first been done in 1965.

Latching on to the popularity of the Daleks, it was decided that Doctor Who would run a 12-part story, The Daleks' Master Plan, which was written by their creator Terry Nation, and Dennis Spooner.

The seventh episode of the story, The Feast of Steven, was shown on Christmas Day 1965, and took a break from the epic Dalek tale, instead giving Nation – a former writer for comedian Tony Hancock – the chance to write a fun one-off episode that was lighter in tone.

It took the TARDIS to Liverpool in the 1960s, then 1920s Hollywood, where the Doctor, Steven and new companion Sara Kingdom – played by future Upstairs Downstairs star Jean Marsh – became involved in the making of a film.

However, The Feast of Steven is unique in Doctor Who history as the episode was never copied onto film for overseas sales, due to the festive nature of the episode, and the only copy of the story was destroyed when the BBC wiped the original videotape to reuse it in the late 1960s.

The Mirror was there to take exclusive pictures of Jean Marsh on set for The Feast of Steven,

NOTHING NEGATIVE:
Jean Marsh on set to film The Feast of Steven

with the majority of these pictures never having been seen before.

Film copies of the other episodes were made for overseas sales, but the story was deemed too scary by censors in Australia for it to be shown there.

Peter Purves, who played Steven, said: "I gather it was one they never sold abroad. I know that the seventh episode was never sold abroad, because it was the Christmas one – that one ended with Bill Hartnell turning to the camera and said 'Merry Christmas to all of you at home'!

"Because they weren't sold abroad, they've disappeared – but I know there's a chance it could be found – it's a 12-part epic. They found an episode about 10 years ago, in the collection of a former BBC employee."

Story editor Donald Tosh, who joined the series late in its second season, worked alongside Verity Lambert's successor John Wiles. The pair had their own plans about what to do with the series, but were given an epic surprise soon after they started work.

Now in his late 70s, Donald recalled: "The most extraordinary thing was, when we came in the scripts for the next few stories were underway, and one of them was a 12-part Dalek story, which we hadn't been told about! We had been working out our own stories before we learned

there was this huge story with the Daleks in it.

"And it was just chaos to do, as Terry Nation was so busy with other things. He was working on a programme he had created, The Baron, which was being made in Hollywood.

"He was getting ready to fly out there, and we were still waiting for his finished scripts to arrive. He phoned up and said he would drop them off at my flat, so I breathed a sigh of relief.

"A while later, the bell went, and Terry handed me an envelope. I was holding a very thin envelope, which was supposed to be six episodes of Doctor Who, and off he went.

"I opened it up, and inside were something like 24 pages of camera directions and a rough storyline, and I just thought, 'Jesus, what am I going to do with this?'

"I rushed out and phoned Johnny and told him the good news, that Terry had delivered his script, and then the bad news, that it was just 24 pages for the six episodes. He just said, 'Good God, Donald... you're going to be very busy!'

"Thankfully, Dougie Camfield the director, the other writer Dennis Spooner, Terry, Johnny and myself had spent a lot of time together to work out the story in advance, so I knew exactly how it should go.

"All the dialogue of those first few episodes was written by me."

FRIENDS AND ENEMIES: The bald-headed Teknix pose with William Hartnell in 1965

THE ARK

New monsters, the Monoids, turn their masters into slaves – but fail to win over co-star Peter Purves

Doctor Who was always looking to create new and successful monsters to follow in the metaphorical footsteps of the Daleks.

Many tried – the Voord, the Sensorites, the Zarbi and the Drahvins to name but four – but none succeeded.

Broadcast in early 1966, The Ark introduce another new monster, the Monoids. The creatures were one-eyed reptiles, who were originally humanity's servants, before turning against their masters and turning the last members of the human race into their slaves.

However, the Monoids didn't make a lasting impression on actor Peter Purves, who appeared in the story as Steven Taylor.

He said: "They were dreadful – a poor realisation of what they wanted to do in this story.

"They looked like a man in a rubber suit with a bad wig on, and a ping-pong ball in their mouth – because that's exactly what they were.

"The story itself was terrific, although there was a bit of serendipity with the TARDIS going back to exactly the same place it had been, 100 years later!"

EYE FOR DANGER: The Doctor's companion Dodo is captured by a Monoid (right) while (top) Handmaidens gather around another

THE GUNFIGHTERS

Although the TARDIS tended to make the majority of its landings on Earth in the British Isles, it has occasionally taken the Doctor and his friends across the pond.

After a fleeting visit to New York in The Chase, 1966's The Gunfighters saw the Doctor, Steven and their new travelling companion Dodo, played by Jackie Lane, land in the Wild West, and became caught up with Wyatt Earp, Doc Holliday and the gunfight at the OK Corral in Tombstone, Arizona.

Unusually, the story featured a musical number, which was performed by Lynda Baron, later known as Nurse Gladys Emmanuel in the BBC comedy series Open All Hours.

However, Peter Purves also had the chance to sing The Ballad of the Last Chance Saloon in the story, which came as a surprise to him.

He laughed: "I definitely didn't expect a musical Western number!

"I didn't enjoy it particularly at the time, but I like it much more nowadays.

"It's a very good piece. The director Rex Tucker

Surprise musical makeover as the TARDIS lands in the Wild West for famous a stand-off

did a brilliant job on it. It's beautifully made, and if we could have done it with the technical expertise they have now, it would have been amazing.

"Unfortunately, we had to record in the Riverside Studios, which weren't the biggest in the world. It's tiny."

The story was covered by the Mirror, which was there to take exclusive pictures during the rehearsals.

The following story, The Savages, saw Peter leave the TARDIS, but he admits that he's delighted to have been involved in three hugely popular British TV series over the years.

He added: "I'm very proud of the fact that I've been involved with three long-running, famous British TV programmes. Not only was I in Doctor Who, I had a great time on Blue Peter, and I also had 13 years doing Kick Start."

LAST CHANCE SALOON: William Hartnell and Sheena Marsh who plays Kate, pictured in a hold-up scene in a Western Saloon Bar, while (bottom right) Peter Purves, who plays Steven Taylor, joins Sheena and Jackie in rehearsals

IN THE EYES OF THE
LAW: William Hartnell
and John Alderson
who played Wyatt
Earp

The War Machines

Invasions of Earth are a staple of Doctor Who, as long-term fans of the series know.

But 1966's The War Machines is an important story as in many ways it shaped what was to come in the eras of the future Doctors, especially his second and third incarnations. The story was set in the contemporary age, and featured a menace trying to take over the world, an approach that was used to great success in Patrick Troughton's The Web of Fear and The Invasion, and became the basis of stories for the majority of Jon Pertwee's time as the Third Doctor.

The War Machines features the computer WOTAN (Will Operating Thought ANalogue), which was installed inside the then-new Post Office Tower (now the BT Tower). WOTAN was able to control the minds of human beings, getting them to build War Machines, which rampaged around London.

WOTAN was also way ahead of its time, pre-empting the internet by decades, as it was communicating with other computers around the world.

These images were taken in May 1966, when William Hartnell took part in some location filming on the streets of London. Interestingly, in our image featuring Hartnell, he is pictured

confronting a War Machine with actor William Mervyn – the father of Michael Pickwoad, who designed Matt Smith's second TARDIS control room.

For several years, The War Machines was thought to have become one of Doctor Who's lost stories, but prints of all four episodes were recovered from a television station in Nigeria in 1984, although they were edited.

When it came to releasing the story on DVD, some of the cuts were able to be restored after clips from the story, which had been removed, were located in an old edition of Blue Peter, along with some clips which were found in the 1990s that had been removed by censors in Australia.

THE
DALEK MOVIES

In the 1950s, 60s and 70s, there was a popular tradition in British television and film: if there was a successful TV series, a film company would adapt it for the big screen.

It regularly occurred with the likes of Quatermass, Steptoe and Son, On The Buses, and Are You Being Served?

And Doctor Who was no exception.

It made perfect sense to take the Daleks and bring them into full colour for the first time, as until then they had only been seen in black and white on British televisions.

With William Hartnell tied up recording the TV series, horror legend Peter Cushing was cast in the part of the Doctor. The storyline of the first Dalek story on TV was used as the basis for the film, Doctor Who and the Daleks, although the Doctor was a human inventor, accompanied by his granddaughters Barbara (Jenny Linden) and Susan (Roberta Tovey), and Barbara's new boyfriend Ian (Roy Castle).

Released in 1965, it was a big enough hit to spawn a sequel, which was based on the second TV Dalek story, The Dalek Invasion of Earth.

As with the first film, it borrowed heavily from the television original, but Daleks: Invasion Earth 2150AD was more action packed, with the Doctor and Susan now being joined by the Doctor's niece Louise (Jill Curzon) and policeman Tom Campbell (Bernard Cribbins).

Cribbins would later star as a regular in the TV series, playing Wilfred Mott, grandfather of Donna Noble (Catherine Tate), who accompanied the Tenth Doctor David Tennant.

The second Dalek film was released in 1966, but by this time interest in the Daleks was on the wane, and plans for an adaptation of the third TV Dalek serial The Chase were dropped.

Cushing would later record a pilot episode of a radio adaptation of Doctor Who for Stanmark Productions in the 1960s, but this was never given a commercial release and no copies of the play are known to exist.

And while Peter Cushing may not be considered as an official TV Doctor, fans still recognise his contribution to the worlds of Doctor Who – and for showing that the Doctor could be successfully played by another actor, not just William Hartnell.

NEW BOY: School children get a close-up view of the Daleks at Shepperton Film Studios in 1965 before they were transported to the Cannes Film Festival, while (left) Roy Castle and Jenny Linden have fun with the Daleks

THE MOONBASE

Villainous Cybermen created in an hour but their evil evolution has seen them come a long way since their sticky tape days

Doctor Who's evil villains the Cybermen were designed in only an hour – and originally held together by sticky tape and safety pins.

The Doctor's second greatest enemies were designed by Alexandra Tynan – and like Raymond Cusick, the designer of the Daleks, she hasn't received an extra penny for her distinctive work, which included their handle-bar head design.

The original Cybermen faced off against William Hartnell in his final story, The Tenth Planet, in 1966. Alexandra revealed to the Mirror in 2006: "No psychological or research work went into it at all. I had to come up with something quickly.

"It wasn't quite designed on the back of a coffee-stained envelope, but it was a bit of a scribble. I had an hour to do a drawing."

The Cybermen were redesigned numerous times over the years, but Sandra's design has always remained as a fan of the classic series.

However, Sandra revealed she didn't want to work on the then-three-year-old hit sci-fi show, even when co-writer Kit Pedler described the show's new robot foes to rival The Daleks.

"He explained the whole idea to me about Cybernetics, which of course in those days nobody had really heard much about," recalled Alexandra, then aged only 25 and using her maiden name Sandra Reid. "The idea was that Cybermen had once been human and had started to change their bodies into replacement parts.

"It was a completely new concept for me. Kit and I chatted to develop the idea and I really didn't want to do the show at all – but I got stuck with it."

The tiny budget caused problems for the poor actors, who wore a thick, stretched body stocking with a polythene suit and plastic ribs on top.

"When I look at those first costumes, they are absolutely dreadful! But we had no money and you just had to do what you could with sticky tape and safety pins," said Alexandra.

"It was a nightmare for these guys to get into these suits. They used to lose quite a bit of weight, but I tried to make them more comfortable.

"There was some fainting as there was no kind of air conditioning and some actors would feel sick and dizzy. I felt awful about it."

The Cybermen returned in 1967 to battle Second Doctor Patrick Troughton in The Moonbase, pictured here, and they were given a redesign.

CYBER PACE:
A young fan accompanies some Cybermen during a break from filming Moonbase at BBC Ealing studios

The Abominable Snowmen

Doctor Who's fifth year saw Patrick Troughton and his companions face off against many monsters.

One of the most popular were the Yeti, which appeared in 1967's The Abominable Snowmen, in which the creatures were revealed to be the robotic servants of the Great Intelligence, an alien entity intending to take control of the planet.

The six-episode story guest-starred Jack Watling, father of actress Deborah, who played the Doctor's companion, Victoria Waterfield.

And years before Doctor Who's production base moved to Cardiff, this story was filmed on location in Snowdonia in Wales, doubling for the Himalayas.

The Yeti proved so popular with the viewers of the time that a second story featuring them was quickly commissioned, The Web of Fear.

SHELTER FROM TERRAIN: Patrick Troughton takes cover from the Welsh weather with the Yeti monsters during filming of The Abominable Snowmen in Snowdonia

"I was surprised they came back actually," admits Belfast-born Alexandra, "but I became more attached to them. They were now sleeker, but the materials then were still very limited."

Despite her monumental contribution, because she was a BBC staff member, she received no more than her regular £22-a-week during her one-year stay on the show. "It was par for the course – I just got my wages. I've never made anything out of it," Alexandra shrugged.

Alexandra admitted she had a "quiet glow" about the influence she had on the legendary show. And she was hooked on the "absolutely brilliant" revived 21st century series.

She added: "The new Cybermen have gone through an amazing transformation. They look a fantastic design.

"Doctor Who was a fabulous experience for me. If I had any idea that Doctor Who was going to haunt me for the rest of my life, I would have maybe come at it from another angle.

"But the surprise has been lovely. I've opened up newspapers recently to see my Cybermen. I was so chuffed. I never realised Doctor Who would crawl back into my life."

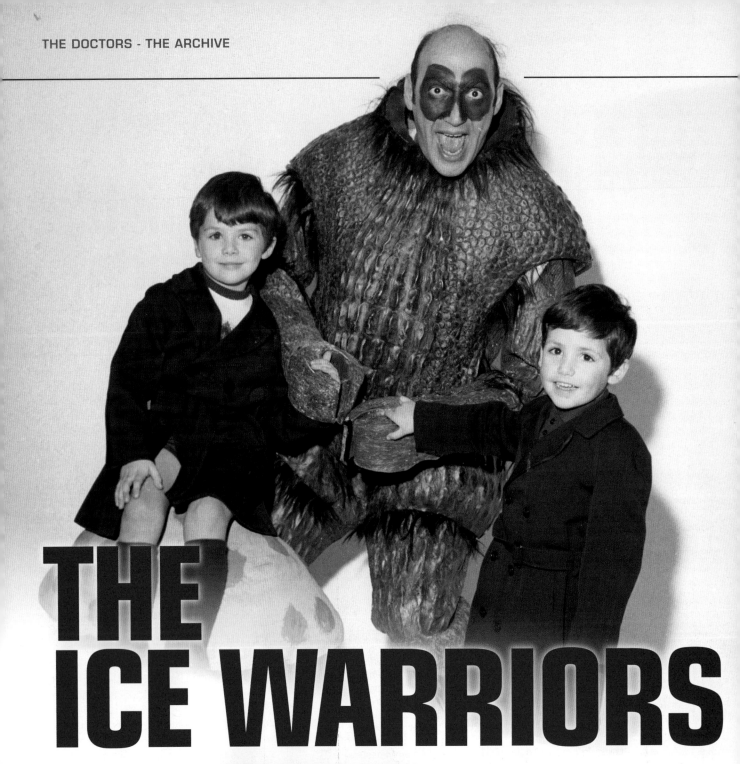

THE ICE WARRIORS

Visitors from Mars bring more monster mayhem with chilling appearances

NO ICE SCREAM: Actor and comedian Bernard Bresslaw, who played the original Ice Warrior leader, doesn't scare his seven-year-old son James

Not only were the Yeti a success in the show's fifth season, they were immediately followed by another monster which would go on to become another series regular.

The Ice Warriors were originally found trapped inside the frozen wastes of a future Ice Age, after their spaceship from Mars had crashed on Earth.

Playing the original Ice Warrior leader was actor Bernard Bresslaw, best known for his appearances in the Carry On films.

He developed the creatures' distinctive rasping, whispering voice, which remained with them afterwards, including their reappearance in 2013 with Matt Smith in The Cold War.

Blue Peter design a monster

Over the years, Doctor Who has regularly featured on another of the BBC's longest-running television programmes – Blue Peter.

In 1967, Blue Peter ran a Design A Monster competition, where young viewers were encouraged to design their own creature which would be tough enough to beat the Daleks and have a secret weapon never before featured on Doctor Who.

Over 250,000 entries were received by the Blue Peter office.

The winners were announced on the December 14 1967 edition of that year. They were the Steel Octopus (designed by Karen Dag in the seven-and-under age group), the Hypnotron (invented by Paul Worrall in the eight to 10 years category), and the Aqua Man (created by Steven Thompson), in the 11 years and over age group).

The creatures were built by the BBC's visual effects department, who created the creatures from the show, and the children were invited to the Blue Peter studio to see their creations brought to life – and also got to meet Second Doctor Patrick Troughton.

Unfortunately for the youngsters, their monstrosities never appeared in Doctor Who itself.

When Doctor Who returned in 2005, executive producer Russell T Davies repeated the idea, except this time the monster did appear in the series.

The winner was the Abzorbaloff, designed by nine-year-old William Grantham, and when it appeared in the 2006 episode Love & Monsters, it was played by comedian Peter Kay.

YOUNG INVENTORS: Blue Peter viewers with their creations

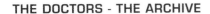

THE WEB

In October 2013, Doctor Who fans were given a treat they never expected – the recovery of nine previously lost episodes from the Patrick Troughton years.

One complete story, The Enemy of the World, was returned to the BBC archives after film prints were found in Nigeria, while four missing episodes from the adventure that followed it, The Web of Fear, were also recovered.

During the filming of episode four of The Web of Fear, the Mirror was there as a group of four Yeti rampaged through the backstreets of London, near Goodge Street underground station in December 1967.

The Yeti were played by actors Gordon

UNWELCOME VISITORS: The Yeti take over London in The Web of Fear

OF FEAR

Rampaging Yeti brought back to life with the discovery of long lost Troughton episodes

Stothard, John Lord, Colin Warman and John Levene (later to play Sergeant Benton with the Second, Third and Fourth Doctors), wearing suits made from Yak fur and wool, with eyes that lit up.

After the BBC wiped the master tapes of the episodes, and all film prints were thought to have been withdrawn, deaccessioned and junked, The Web of Fear was thought lost forever, until the efforts of Philip Morris returned the prints from Africa to the UK. Although Patrick Troughton sadly passed away in 1987, his companions in the story Frazer Hines and Deborah Watling, playing Jamie McCrimmon and Victoria Waterfield, revealed their delight at viewing the recovered episodes for only the second time ever.

For Debbie, it was a special story to see, as she acted opposite her late father, Jack, playing Professor Travers.

But she admitted that she and Frazer initially didn't believe the news about the discovery of the episodes.

She said: "I thought 'no, this is ridiculous – there's been so many rumours over the years'."

FURRY FRIENDS: Some urban dogs get a surprise when they encounter The Yeti during filming of The Web of Fear near Goodge Street underground station in 1967

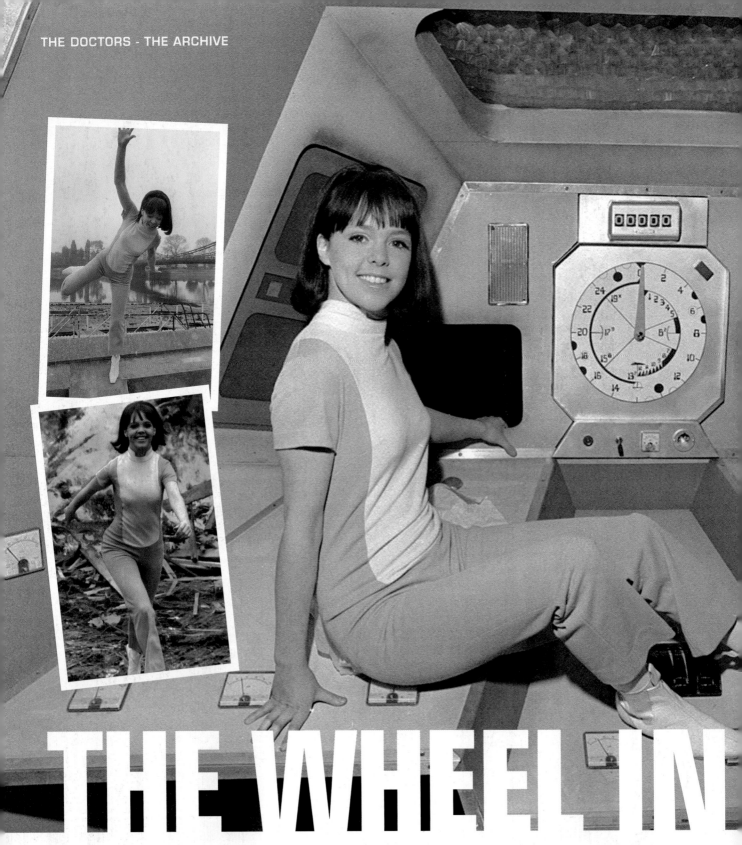

THE WHEEL IN

ACTION GIRL:
Wendy Padbury on the photoshoot to announce her role as Zoe Heriot, the latest companion of Second Doctor Patrick Troughton

The final story of Doctor Who's fifth season saw the arrival of a stowaway in the TARDIS.

Plucky young astrophysicist Zoe Heriot (Wendy Padbury) had helped the Doctor and Jamie defeat the Cybermen, who had tried to take control of The Wheel in Space. At the end of the story, she snuck into the TARDIS and hid inside a chest, but was found by the time travellers. They agreed to let her join them on their adventures.

Wendy said: "It was a very strange time – I'd got the part, was given my costume, and I felt very grown up when I was taken to do my photoshoot – it was very exciting for me.

"I don't think we would have done it a million miles away from the BBC.

Young stowaway thrust into the spotlight as she joins the Doctor on his space travels

"I do remember the shoot, though, as that outfit I wore had been specially made for it, and I went on to wear it in my first story.

"The shoot itself was amazing, as it was all a bit new to me. I'd never done a job before where you had your pictures taken before you'd even started working. It all seemed very grand to me at that time."

Like many other stories from the Patrick Troughton era of Doctor Who, The Wheel in Space isn't complete in the BBC archives, as only

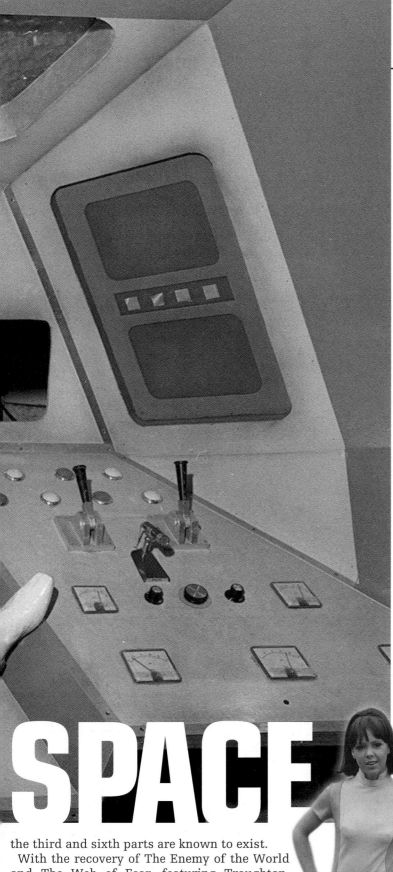

HOME COMFORT:
Wendy takes time out
from filming in 1968

SPACE

'I'd got the part, was given my costume, and I felt very grown up when I was taken to do my photoshoot'

the third and sixth parts are known to exist.

With the recovery of The Enemy of the World and The Web of Fear, featuring Troughton, Frazer Hines and Wendy's predecessor Deborah Watling, she is optimistic that one day The Wheel in Space might be seen again in full.

BBC sales records show that it was sold to Nigeria around the same time that the recently-recovered episodes were.

Wendy added: "Who knows? The BBC might already have them.

"The problem with missing episodes is similar to the way things were in those years when Doctor Who was off the air for so long – every six months or so, you'd hear it was going to come back, and it wasn't the case.

"Now, you hear all these rumours that they've found missing episodes, and for years, nothing happened, then all of a sudden these episodes show up. I was really pleased for Debbie Watling, as so few of hers survived. She lost more episodes than anyone.

"It's all very exciting – we can but hope!"

In 1974, Wendy was given the chance to play another companion, when she took on the role of Jenny, in the stageplay Doctor Who and the Daleks in the Seven Keys to Doomsday. Wendy would briefly reappear as Zoe in the 20th anniversary special The Five Doctors. She also had a spell in Emmerdale Farm, where she worked alongside her old Doctor Who sparring partner Frazer Hines.

THE THIRD DOCTOR

Unlikely choice Pertwee makes lead role his own

When Jon Pertwee was cast as the Third Doctor, it wasn't the most obvious piece of casting.

Until then, Pertwee was best known as a radio voice actor, appearing in a number of hit shows including the Navy Lark, as well as small guest roles in several Carry On films.

When he was told he had got the part of the Doctor, Pertwee asked how he should play the Time Lord, and his producer told him to play it as himself. Having been used to wearing wigs and glasses throughout his career, he replied: "As Jon Pertwee? Who on Earth is that?"

Jon had a love of gadgets and motor vehicles, and was able to introduce them into the show.

The Pertwee era initially saw a change in emphasis on Doctor Who, leaving alien planets behind as the Doctor was exiled to Earth by the Time Lords. This was partly a cost-saving measure, as the show moved from black and white into colour, and with fewer episodes in each season.

Over the course of his five years as the Doctor, the Pertwee era introduced a number of elements which would recur over the years, with many of them appearing again in the 21st century version of Doctor Who – the Autons, the Nestenes, the Master, the Silurians, the Sontarans and companion Sarah Jane Smith.

After leaving Doctor Who, Jon would later be cast as Worzel Gummidge, bringing the friendly scarecrow to life on ITV.

In his later years, Pertwee became a regular on the Doctor Who convention circuit, appearing in his distinctive costume with frilly shirt and cape, and proudly proclaiming on stage: "I am the Doctor!"

He also made a record, also called I am the Doctor, before returning to play the Doctor in the 20th anniversary special The Five Doctors, on stage in 1989 in The Ultimate Adventure, then in two radio plays, The Paradise of Death and The Ghosts of N-Space.

Sadly, Jon Pertwee died, aged 76, in May 1996 after suffering a heart attack. When the Doctor Who TV Movie starring Paul McGann aired a week later, it was dedicated to his memory.

BEING HIMSELF:
Jon Pertwee pictured at home in the early 1970s

DAY OF THE DALEKS

Pertwee takes to the streets to promote ninth series

In 1967, Dalek creator Terry Nation decided that he wanted to try and launch the Daleks in a TV series of their own.

A script was written for a pilot episode, The Destroyers, but this was ultimately never made for television, although an audio adaptation was released in 2010.

As a result, Nation reeled in all Dalek stories, meaning the BBC were unable to do new stories on TV with the Doctor, and it looked as if Patrick Troughton's second encounter with them in The Evil of the Daleks, would be their final story.

Nation also stopped the BBC from selling old Dalek serials overseas, which meant very few countries got to see their meetings with the Second Doctor.

However, things changed for the first story of Doctor Who's ninth season, when his oldest foes returned in Day of the Daleks.

It saw the Daleks invade Earth in the future, and human rebels travelled back in time to stop them. However, working with the Doctor, the rebels were able to foil the Dalek invasion.

To promote the return of the Daleks, Jon Pertwee took part in a photocall on the streets of London.

Pertwee was very vocal in his dislike of working with the Daleks.

He far preferred to work with other actors whom he could look in the eye, citing creatures like the Draconians and the Ogrons as being of more interest to him.

'Jon Pertwee was very vocal in his dislike of working with Daleks. Creatures like the Draconians and the Ogrons were of more interest to him'

THE WHOMOBILE

During his five-year reign as the Doctor, Jon Pertwee was able to bring his personal love of unusual vehicles and gadgets into the show.

As the Doctor, Jon was seen to enjoy several vehicles in addition to his vintage car Bessie, including riding a motorised tricycle, piloting a helicopter and driving a speedboat.

However, arguably the most unusual vehicle he drove was a machine Jon Pertwee commissioned himself from car customiser Peter Farries. The car became known to fans as the Whomobile.

This vehicle, which appeared to be like a hovercraft, featured in the 1974 stories Invasion of the Dinosaurs and Planet of the Spiders. Pertwee regularly told fans at conventions of how he was regularly pulled over by the police while driving it, and it was actually registered as an invalid tricycle.

The car was officially known as Alien, but on TV, the Doctor only ever referred to it as "my car".

Prior to his death in 1996, Pertwee gifted the vehicle to a fan.

Pertwee's customised ride attracted plenty of attention

DOCTOR ON CALL: *Jon Pertwee in his personally commissioned car, which was capable of speeds in excess of 100mph and was equipped with a computer, TV, telephone and stereo*

The Time Warrior

When actress Elisabeth Sladen joined Doctor Who as new companion Sarah Jane Smith in 1973, little did she realise how much her life was about to change.

Sarah Jane became the Doctor's longest-running companion, witnessing Jon Pertwee's regeneration into Tom Baker in June 1974, before finally leaving his side in October 1976.

Lis brought the investigative journalist to life with vigour and passion, making Sarah Jane the most popular companion of the classic series.

But the actress didn't realise that she would be back in the part several times over the years. She returned in the pilot episode for an aborted spin-off K9 and Company, featuring the Doctor's robot dog companion, broadcast in December 1981, and again for the 20th anniversary special The Five Doctors in November 1983.

But in March 2005, Sarah Jane Smith won herself a whole legion of new fans when she returned in the second season of the 21st century revival of Doctor Who. Her meeting with David Tennant in the story School Reunion was so popular that it led to the creation of a new spin-off series, the Sarah Jane Adventures, for Children's BBC.

The Sarah Jane Adventures ran for five series.

Sadly, Elisabeth Sladen passed away in April 2011, aged just 65. Her passing made headline news, showing the affection with which the character – and actress – were held.

TWO DOCTORS AND A LADY: Lis Sladen pictured with the Doctors she worked with – Jon Pertwee (above) and Tom Baker (right)

Doctor Who and the Daleks in the Seven Keys to Doomsday

In the long months between Jon Pertwee regenerating into Tom Baker, before the 12th series of Doctor Who aired, there was a 'lost' Doctor.

Trevor Martin, who had played a Time Lord in Patrick Troughton's final TV story The War Games, received the ultimate promotion, by taking on the role of the Doctor for the stageplay Doctor Who and the Daleks in the Seven Keys to Doomsday in 1974.

The show was written by Terrance Dicks, and ran at the Adelphi Theatre in London, for four weeks, starting on December 16.

Trevor's Doctor was accompanied by a familiar face, with another veteran of the Troughton years, Wendy Padbury, playing a new companion, Jenny.

Writer Terrance Dicks said of the original stage play and Trevor Martin: "It was great fun – he's a nice fellow and he was faced with an impossible job in taking over from one of the 'real' Doctors, in Jon, and he did very well."

Sadly, plans to take the show on a national tour collapsed after a series of terrorist bombings in London.

However, the play was adapted for audio by Big Finish Productions, with Trevor Martin returning to the part of the Doctor, and actress Charlie Hayes, the daughter of Wendy Padbury, taking over her mum's old role as Jenny.

ROAD SHOW: Trevor Martin prepares for the Doctor Who stage production by getting to grips with the archenemy outside the Adelphi Theatre in London where it ran for four weeks

When Tom Baker was cast as the Fourth Doctor, no one could have possibly imagined the impact he would have on the role.

After five years as the Doctor, Jon Pertwee looked as if he would be impossible to replace, but producer Barry Letts struck gold when he gave the part to the tall, curly-haired, rich-voiced former monk from Liverpool.

A stroke of fortune came the way of the production team when they were settling on a look for the new Doctor, as they wanted him to wear a scarf and provided a load of wool to witty little knitter Begonia Pope. Rather than knit several shorter scarves, she instead used all the wool and the result became a TV legend!

Even now, in the 21st century, despite all the unique and distinctive outfits that have followed Tom's, his is still the one that most endures, with the long scarf and floppy hat. Such was his impact that the Fourth Doctor often appeared in the background in episodes of The Simpsons!

When Tom was introduced to the press in 1974, he was relatively unknown to the mass audience.

At his first photocall, he was joined by Elisabeth Sladen, who was staying on as Sarah Jane Smith, and the two Scousers very quickly formed a close bond of friendship, which was to last for decades. They were accompanied by a Cyberman, just to ensure there was a menace for the new Doctor on his first day in the job!

Soon after, a second photocall was held when Tom's new costume was established, and he and Elisabeth were accompanied by another newcomer to the TARDIS, Royal Navy medic Harry Sullivan, played by Ian Marter.

THE FOURTH DOCTOR

Former Liverpool monk brings Time Lord his most distinguished look

In their first year together, they faced the Sontarans, the Daleks and the Cybermen, and after an encounter with the Zygons in Scotland, Harry returned to his medical life.

However, the Doctor and Sarah Jane continued on their adventures for many more months, before Lis decided to move on to pastures new.

But for Lis Sladen and Sarah Jane Smith, the end was only just the beginning...

Tom would go on to play the Doctor for a total of seven years, a total which has never since been broken by any of his successors, before he finally hung up his scarf in 1980.

TERROR OF THE ZYGONS

LET ZYGONS BE ZYGONS: Tom Baker went to West Sussex to film an episode about the Loch Ness monster

When the TARDIS brought the Doctor and his friends back to Scotland, they ended up facing the Loch Ness monster.

Terror of the Zygons starred Tom Baker as the Fourth Doctor, which was written by Robert Banks Stewart, and broadcast in 1975.

Robert, now 82, was a reporter for the Daily Mirror before taking up writing for television.

Although he only wrote for Doctor Who twice, Robert has a lengthy and proud list of TV credits, including creating hit detective shows Shoestring and Bergerac.

Robert, now living in London, said: "I was very friendly with Patrick Troughton, the Second Doctor, and we used to play golf together, but I never wrote a script for him.

"My sons nagged me and said, 'Come on, why don't you write a Doctor Who?' At the time, Philip Hinchcliffe was the producer on Doctor Who, and one day he just said, 'Come on, why don't you write one?'

"So I wrote Terror of the Zygons. I'm not good at doing things which are set in outer space, and

I said I'd rather do one that was set on Earth. I suggested I do one about the Loch Ness monster, where we find out it's really an alien, and there's an underground river which leads from Loch Ness to the sea, that no one knows about.

"There were also aliens, and I thought the guy who is the Laird should be another space alien – I thought it was a nice idea, the Highland Laird, wearing his kilt and drinking his malt whisky, but is from outer space. It was a lot of fun."

Although a Scot was writing a story set in Scotland, when it came to location filming, the BBC crew doing the shoot unfortunately didn't make it across the border.

Robert explained: "We couldn't go to Scotland to shoot it, so in the end we went down to West Sussex. They managed to do a decent job of it, making it look like Scotland.

"Back in those days, there was no CGI (computer generated imagery) or anything like that – they had to use puppets and stop-motion animation, and I think it was okay for the time."

The shape-changing Zygons won themselves many fans, but despite their popularity, didn't

appear in the series again, although they are due to show up in the show's 50th anniversary special episode, The Name of the Doctor. However, they did have some famous fans.

Robert said: "I was later told by someone that some of the Royal children had watched it and enjoyed it, possibly Prince Edward, and had said it was their favourite story."

Another admirer of Terror of the Zygons is Tenth Doctor David Tennant, who has gone on record as saying that the Zygons were his favourite Doctor Who monsters.

Robert laughed: "I never knew that! Thank you, David."

Although Robert has now retired, last year he returned to writing with a novel, The Hurricane's Tail, a crime thriller ranging from London and Paris to the Caribbean, with the lead character Harper Buchana, being a West Indian who has never set foot in the West Indies.

Robert said: "None of the major book publishers wanted it, so it was picked up by a smaller firm. I had hoped it would be picked up and turned into a TV series. We will see!"

"Back in those days there was no CGI – they had to use puppets and stop-motion animation, and I think it was okay for the time"

THE FACE OF EVIL

Latest companion felt alienated during early days with the Doctor

I n 1977, Tom Baker was not a happy man.
With Elisabeth Sladen having left his side
as Sarah Jane Smith after two-and-a-half
years as his companion, Tom felt that the
Doctor should travel alone for a while, and if he
had to have a companion, it should be a talking
cabbage that would sit on his shoulder.

Tom didn't get his way, and instead, Louise
Jameson was cast as his new sidekick, Leela,
a savage from an alien world in the future, a
descendant of a crashed Earth colony ship.

However, it wasn't a happy job for Louise at
first, as she initially found her co-star difficult.

She said: "We didn't really connect in the 1970s.
Nowadays, I absolutely adore him and I love
working with him when we do the Big Finish
audio stories.

"I think he's intelligent, witty, kind, giving, and
I so look forward to seeing him because I know
I'm going to have a laugh. He's 80 in January, and

ALIEN ATTRACTION: The Doctor and his new assistant, Leela, played by Louise Jameson

'We didn't really connect in the 1970s. Nowadays, I absolutely adore him and I love working with him when we do the Big Finish audio stories'

an incredible man. That's everyone's reaction to him – he's a wonderful man.

"But back then, I never thought I would be saying those things, because he gave me such a hard time. Thankfully, though, he's apologised for it, and he regrets it deeply – he's just a great man."

Louise, who later played Rosa di Marco in EastEnders, was given a skimpy leather outfit to wear, as the primitive Leela, who quickly impressed the Doctor with her quick thinking and ability to adapt to new situations.

Louise recalled of her introduction as Leela: "It actually felt like it was someone else that day. It was the first time I'd been blasted by bright flashing lights like that.

"I was taught, when someone calls out your name at these things, don't turn round and look

at them. I was told you just very slowly move your head round, so everyone can get a shot, from their different angles. If you move too quickly from one side to the other, no one is going to get a good shot. As a 20-odd something, I really rather enjoyed it.

"It was a very odd day – it started early as I was in make-up at 7am and was there in the studio until 11 at night, rehearsing all morning and then stopping for the photoshoot at lunchtime, then having a dinner break later in the day before recording, and I also went on Nationwide that night!

"I don't think I found it that daunting – it was EastEnders I found far more daunting when I did that, many years later, at the turn of the century. Maybe it was the way the press had become more intrusive over the years."

On the big screen in 1977, Star Wars introduced two iconic robots (or droids) in the form of R2D2 and C3PO. After them, machines in science fiction would never be the same again.

In the Doctor Who universe, 1977 saw the arrival of a Time Lord's best friend, with K9 arriving in the TARDIS.

Originally, K9 was a one-off character in The Invisible Enemy, but the production team took a real shine to the dog and added him to the regular line-up. K9 was created by the late Dave Martin, and Bob Baker – the future Oscar-winning writer of Wallace and Gromit.

Tom Baker was vociferous in his dislike of the dog, as he was constantly having to drop down to ground level to talk with the machine, saving his praise instead for the actor who voiced the metal mutt, John Leeson.

His co-star Louise Jameson said: "With K9 arriving, it was lovely John Leeson who was the real unsung hero.

"In that first photoshoot we did with K9, I nearly caused an accident as some shots were being taken outside the Acton Hilton, as we called the rehearsal rooms, as there were some big trucks going past and there was me with my costume on – it caught their eye!

"We didn't have the prop K9 when we were in the rehearsal room, as we couldn't afford to have it there. It was one of those crazy situations where the BBC had to hire from itself!

"Instead, we had John Leeson going down on all fours, playing the dog, and that really worked to our advantage. We had this wonderful relationship with John in the rehearsal room, and we tried to carry it on in the studio when they brought out the tin box."

K9 continued to appear in Doctor Who in 1980, until he was written out. However, it wasn't the end, as another model of the dog was gifted to Sarah Jane Smith, featuring in an aborted pilot episode for a spin-off series, K9 and Company, in 1980. K9 later returned in the 20th anniversary special, and in 1990 featured alongside Seventh Doctor Sylvester McCoy in a children's TV programme Search Out Science.

The dog made a proper return to Doctor Who in 2006, opposite David Tennant, once again at the side of Sarah Jane Smith, before being destroyed, but a new K9 mark IV was presented to Sarah Jane – with K9 appearing in her spin-off series The Sarah Jane Adventures. A separate Australian K9 series was also made, featuring a brand new design of the dog, having been devised by his original co-creator Bob Baker.

Although his cute design has made K9 a hit with viewers, one man who has been there for K9 since day one is John Leeson, who also voiced him in the Australian series.

Louise added: "I really think John is the single reason why K9 was so successful.

"He once went to a convention in America, but because he wasn't seen onscreen, no one knew what he looked like. He took part in a K9 soundalike competition – and came second!"

The Invisible Enemy

METAL MUTT: Tom Baker, Louise Jameson and K9

THE RIBOS OPERATION

Doctor meets his equal as Time Lady brings brains and beauty in the Key to Time

Doctor Who achieved a new level of glamour in 1978, when Mary Tamm was cast as the Doctor's new companion, Romana.

Romana – or Romanadvoratrelundar, to give her her full name – was a Time Lady, fresh from the academy and sent to join the Doctor on his quest to locate the six segments of the Key to Time.

She was more than a match for Tom Baker's Doctor, with her own line in witty put-downs, as well as having the intelligence to match – or indeed better – the Doctor's own.

These pictures feature Mary at her press call with Tom Baker, who is sporting a plaster on his lip, after being bitten in a pub by a dog named George, after offering it a sausage!

Sadly, Mary Tamm passed away in 2012, just weeks after returning to the role of Romana in a series of seven audio dramas, which were released in 2013 by Big Finish Productions.

SOMETHING ABOUT MARY: Mary Tamm gets ready to join the Doctor in her role as Romana

CITY OF DEATH

Series heads to French capital to foil art dealer

For all of Doctor Who's notoriety as being cheaply made in the 20th century, with wobbly sets, it's often forgotten that the series featured overseas filming.

In 1979, City of Death took the Doctor and Romana to Paris, in a story which was written by the legendary Douglas Adams, author of The Hitchhiker's Guide To The Galaxy.

Thanks to some clever budgeting, Tom Baker and Lalla Ward were shown at the Eiffel Tower, the Louvre, Notre Dame, beside the River Seine, travelling on the Metro and on the streets of Paris, as they sought to foil Count Scarlioni, who was selling duplicate copies of the Mona Lisa – which had been painted by Leonardo da Vinci.

Filming took place in May 1979, but unfortunately when Tom Baker rattled the doors of the Louvre – which was closed due to a public holiday in Paris – he set off a burglar alarm, causing the cast and crew to make a quick exit!

As always, the Mirror was there to capture the moment.

FRENCH CONNECTION: Tom Baker and Lalla Ward on location in Paris

51

Lalla becomes Tom Baker's new assistant and the relationship is so strong, the pair get married!

Destiny of the Daleks

Actress Lalla Ward enjoyed a real stroke of luck after appearing in Doctor Who.

Initially, she was cast as Princess Astra for six episodes in the 16th season story The Armageddon Factor.

But she made such a good impression on the cast and crew that when Mary Tamm decided to leave the part of Romana after a year, she regenerated into Lalla.

Lalla – the daughter of Edward Ward, 7th Viscount Bangor – made her on-screen debut in 1979's Destiny of the Daleks, alongside Tom Baker.

The pair grew very close during the recording of the 17th and 18th seasons of the show, and were married in December 1980, just months after both had left Doctor Who. Sadly, the marriage only lasted 16 months.

Lalla is now married to evolutionary biologist Richard Dawkins and occasionally still acts, regularly recreating the part of Romana in BBC-licensed audio dramas from Big Finish Productions.

REGENERATED: Lalla Ward – who became the second actress to play Romana – is pictured (top) with K9 and her own dog in 1979

STATE OF DECAY

As Doctor Who entered the 1980s, the show underwent a massive revamp. With Star Wars ruling the roost at the box office, it had set a new standard in science fiction that Doctor Who could only dare to dream of matching, let alone surpass.

A producer was appointed, and John Nathan-Turner was determined to make the show as glitzy as possible. He commissioned a new version of the show's famous theme tune, had a new title sequence created, gave the show a new logo, and introduced a new companion into the mix.

Joining Tom Baker and Lalla Ward as the Doctor and Romana was young actor Matthew Waterhouse, who was only 18 at the time. He was cast as Adric, and had the credentials of being a proper long-term fan of the show.

Matthew said: "It was tremendously exciting and unexpected. It came completely out of

the blue, so it was surreal and strange too! Nowadays a lot of the writers and actors are big fans of the whole 50 years of Doctor Who, but at that time it was a novelty to have an actor in the series who could name all the stories of ten years earlier!

"I knew more about Tom's stories than he did, but I didn't have the heart to tell him. And all these years later, I, like other Doctor Who actors, am still working on new DW material, in audio dramas and audiobooks, which I didn't imagine in 1980.

"I had always felt like an alien anyway so it made sense that my TV hero should be an alien, and also that when I was cast in the series it was to play an alien! I liked the programme's wildness and imagination and strangeness. For a lot of people, the Rovers Return or the Queen Vic are realistic, but I found the TARDIS easier to believe in! It was very vivid and alive to me, and the element of fear which, at the time, was a big part of DW was very intense and memorable. I think that's why it's lasted – people never forget the things that frighten them. During my time Doctor Who was still famous for causing children sleepless nights."

Matthew, who has written an autobiography entitled Blue Box Boy, recorded his first story, State of Decay, before the adventure in which he made his debut, Full Circle, and he adored the experience.

He added: "I have never forgotten my first day on the TARDIS set. Tom was at the other end of the studio shooting a scene. The TARDIS set was dark and I remember circling it and pulling the levers, and I could hear Tom's voice coming from the other set. It was like I was in a dream. I also remember the thrill of reading my first script, which was a story about vampires by the DW legend Terrance Dicks. I read it, thinking how fantastic it was, and I couldn't quite believe I was being paid money to be in it."

NEW BOY: Matthew Waterhouse joins the cast as Adric

Seeing Double

Tom Baker's popularity as Doctor Who saw him bestowed with the ultimate honour in 1980 – he was transformed into a waxwork at the London Madame Tussauds.

With his curly hair, toothy grin and lengthy scarf, Tom became an iconic figure on both sides of the Atlantic.

So he was delighted when he was copied into a waxwork – giving him plenty of chances to lark about with his duplicate when he came face-to-face with it.

Tom also achieved a unique claim by having two wax versions of himself on show at the same time in Madame Tussauds – not only was his copy as the Doctor on show, there was also a similar version of him as the alien Meglos.

Meglos was the last of the cactus-like Zolpha-Thurans, which took a copy of the Doctor's form, but later degraded to look like a half-man, half-cactus, with this also going on display.

The waxwork dummy was later used to good effect, to promote Doctor Who's 20th anniversary.

THINKING OUTSIDE THE BOX: Peter Davison gets ready for his role as the cricket-loving Fifth Doctor

'I thought it was a brilliant piece of casting to take a younger man and make him the Doctor...back then it was very unusual to have a younger Doctor'

CASTROVALVA

Fifth Doctor explores new boundaries as producer appoints youngest-ever Time Lord to succeed the great Tom Baker

A whole generation of Doctor Who fans have grown up with Tom Baker as the Time Lord.

So it came as a real shock for those who had never heard of regeneration before, as they only knew the man who was all teeth and curls.

When John Nathan-Turner selected Tom's successor, he went for an actor who was already a household name – Peter Davison, who appeared as Tristan Farnon in All Creatures Great and Small.

Davison was also the youngest actor to play the part – as he was just 29 when he was cast.

His costume was a contrast to Tom Baker's, as Nathan-Turner commissioned an outfit based on

an Edwardian cricketer's, which was topped off with a stick of celery on the lapel!

Fiona Cumming directed Peter's first story, Castrovalva.

She said: "He had been doing particularly well on All Creatures Great and Small, and he already had a big following, and I thought it was a brilliant piece of casting to take a younger man and make him the Doctor.

"Nowadays, it's far more common with the likes of David Tennant and Matt Smith as the Doctor, but back then it was very unusual to have a younger Doctor. Until then he had always been an older man, with Bill Hartnell, Patrick Troughton, Jon Pertwee and Tom Baker. He showed it worked."

BACK IN TIME:
A rather unimpressed-looking Peter Davison, along with Sarah Sutton, Janet Fielding and Matthew Watehouse at Buckhurst House in East Sussex in 1981

BLACK ORCHID

After a 15-year break the Doctor goes back in time
– as a stunt man proved the only real fall guy

Doctor Who producers claimed in the show's early days that some stories received higher ratings than others. They were of the belief that the science fiction adventures were more popular with the viewers than the historicals, which had seen the Doctor and his friends encounter characters like Marco Polo, Emperor Nero and Doc Holliday.

As a result, the Doctor was facing alien threats or enemies from within on a weekly basis, with a guest monster invariably appearing every week.

However there was a surprise for viewers in the programme's 19th season, broadcast in March 1982, in the story Black Orchid.

For the first time since The Highlanders in 1967, the Doctor went back in time, and didn't face any monsters at all, in an historical adventure set in an English country house in 1925.

Peter Davison was the Doctor, accompanied by Sarah Sutton as Nyssa, Janet Fielding as Tegan, and Matthew Waterhouse was Adric. It gave them the chance to dress up for the day, for a fancy dress ball.

Matthew said: "Black Orchid was one of the most enjoyable stories to make. A great cast, and they all had a good time on it.

"I saw actor Michael Cochrane recently and he still remembered it fondly. The evenings were spent in a social huddle in a rather dowdy Tunbridge Wells hotel. Much of the story took place outside, at a 1920s garden party, but the weather was rainy and cold.

"There was a table covered in food, including a chicken, which the floor manager kept eating bits of between takes, to the consternation of the set designer.

"One terrible thing happened: the stunt man Gareth Milne had to throw himself off the roof of this old country house. There was a high pile of cardboard boxes to break his fall, but he overshot the boxes and plummeted to the grass. It was a scary moment, but all he had were a few bruises. Stunt men are tough people."

WAXING LYRICAL: The five Doctors including Richard Hurndall – a replacement for William Hartnell – and a waxwork of Tom Baker

The Five Doctors

In 1983, Doctor Who marked its 20th anniversary.

Ten years previously, the first three Doctors were united to face renegade Time Lord Omega in a celebratory story The Three Doctors.

So a decade later, it was decided that the five incarnations of the Time Lord would be brought together to face a new danger.

Unfortunately, though, original Doctor William Hartnell had died in April 1975.

And the problems were compounded when Tom Baker chose not to reprise the role which had made him famous, citing the fact he had only left the part two years beforehand as part of his decision.

So with Patrick Troughton, Jon Pertwee and Peter Davison on board, a replacement for Hartnell was found in veteran actor Richard Hurndall.

When a photocall was held for the show, all five Doctors were present, with Hurndall joining Davison, Pertwee and Troughton - along with the waxwork of Tom Baker from Madame Tussauds!

This gave the other Doctors the chance to have some fun with the dummy as they posed for the Mirror's cameras.

They were also joined by actresses Carole Ann Ford and Elisabeth Sladen, as well as Nicholas Courtney.

PLANET OF FIRE

When Nicola Bryant was cast as the Fifth Doctor's new companion, little did she know she'd be acting on and off the camera.

Nicola was revealed as Perpugilliam Brown – known as Peri – in the summer of 1983, playing the Time Lord's first American companion.

Although Nicola was born and bred in Britain, the show's producer John Nathan-Turner (JNT) actually thought that she came from the other side of the Atlantic.

Nicola said: "He thought I was American because my agent never told him. I was even filmed by an American film crew during the audition and they didn't know. No one did.

"Once cast JNT asked about me doing a dual nationality accent as he thought Peri's father was probably British, although he was dead. This came from an idea that I had that Peter Davison's Doctor could remind Peri of her father and that's why she decides to stay in the TARDIS with him. This was not reflected in the scripts, sadly, so when I was asked to say 'glarce' instead of 'glass' it sounded a little Bostonian as well as British."

At the time, Nicola was married to an American, but her producer wanted her to give the impression that she was single.

Nicola said: "JNT did insist that I pretend to be single – hence my wedding ring is on my other hand. But the American was the fault of my agent, who had seen me in a drama school production doing an American accent and he thought I was genuinely American.

"It was a strange moment for me – it was literally my first job, and I was being asked to be an unmarried American all the time.

"So, all the interviews, everything I did was conducted in an American accent. I guessed that the acting life was always going to be odd!

"I didn't spend a lot of time worrying about it, as I guessed I would just have to keep acting.

"It was a sign of the times, I suppose. Dominic West is a friend of mine, and he didn't have to pretend to be an American to get his part in The Wire.

"I'd actually done all my casting auditions with an American accent, because they said they were only prepared to look at Americans. My agent was supposed to let them know I wasn't American if I got the part but he chickened

New companion Nicola brings an American accent and a flexible wardrobe

out of telling them. John didn't want people to know I was married as he was worried it would interfere with my likeability."

Nicola, in her first job in TV, wasn't too sure what to expect ahead of her first photocall, but JNT wanted to make sure that she grabbed the media's attention.

Nicola said: "Literally two days before the photoshoot, JNT called me up and said we have got the photocall. He then asked me, 'What's the shortest skirt you've got?' I didn't have anything like that, as I had a long white skirt. The lowest I had was just below the knee – it wasn't the 60s!

"He then asked me, what's the shortest thing in your wardrobe, and I told him shorts, which were longer than the ones I ended up wearing.

"Then John asked me, what kind of clinging tops do you have? I told him I didn't think I had anything like that – I had a boob tube, as they were in fashion, but that was it. He wanted to know what else I had, but it was just normal

AMERICAN DREAMS: Nicola Bryant wasn't exactly what producer John Nathan-Turner was expecting

The Twin Dilemma

Sixth Doctor Colin Baker was unveiled to the world in his distinctive costume – a cornucopia of clashing chromatics – in March 1994.

And along with Nicola Bryant, who was with the Doctor when he regenerated from his fifth incarnation, the pair weren't given the most stylish of outfits for their first story together, The Twin Dilemma, broadcast in 1984.

Nicola joked: "I think the two of us were 'abused', as far as costumes went!"

Colin's multi-coloured outfit, which would have put Joseph's Technicolor Dreamcoat to shame, was the result of producer John Nathan-Turner asking costume designer Pat Godfrey to come up with something "totally tasteless."

When the new Doctor and his companion were revealed at their first photocall, poor Nicola was given an outfit which didn't flatter her figure in any way at all.

She recalled of the press conference: "That was my least favourite outfit, because that's not the way it was designed and made. Originally, the blouse had a high collar with buttons down one side of the shoulder and the skirt was mid calf. John saw it in the studio for the first time and went nuts! He was shouting, 'We can't have that!', and gave the costume department an hour to cut two foot off the skirt and hack out the neckline of the blouse, before we started filming, so it never sat right.

"Everything was falling in the wrong place. Even the knee length boots had to be folded over. It doesn't look right at all.

"In those days the BBC had to make everything – even my bikini! I mean, who makes a bikini?"

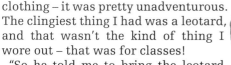

clothing – it was pretty unadventurous. The clingiest thing I had was a leotard, and that wasn't the kind of thing I wore out – that was for classes!

"So he told me to bring the leotard and the shorts, and we would work something out.

"In all the auditions I'd done, I'd worn what a young student would have been wearing, with a lot of sweatshirts, jeans and sneakers. Just before we did the photographs, John handed me a bag of cotton wool and told me to stuff my bra! I said, 'I think you'll find I don't need it.' He hadn't seen me in anything other than baggy sweatshirts until that point.

"At least I wasn't cast for all the things John spent the next three years putting on display!

"It was good to know I'd been cast for my portrayal of Peri, not for other attributes."

THE SIXTH DOCTOR

Playing Doctor Who or one of his many companions means that the actors who bring the parts to life are always in demand.

Actors are always wanted on the convention circuit, not just in Britain, but in places as far flung as America, Australia and New Zealand, demonstrating just how far the series' popularity goes.

Although the actors tended to be out of costume for these events, sometimes they would make personal appearances wearing their Doctor Who uniforms. Colin Baker and Nicola Bryant are shown here in 1985 at Heathrow, before flying out to a convention in Miami.

On May 16 that year Lisa Jenkins, of Neath, is pictured with Colin and a time capsule before it was buried in the foundations of South Glamorgan's new county library in Cardiff.

Eleven-year-old Lisa Jenkins won a competition organised by BBC's Welsh-language children's programme, Biliodowcar.

Even years after leaving the TARDIS, Colin was in demand, being asked along to perform the opening of Cyberzone at Yorkgate in Belfast in March 1999, where he met his match in 16-year-old Diane Rea.

IN DEMAND:
(Left) Colin Baker and Nicola Bryant prepare to fly to a convention in Miami in 1985
(Above) Colin faces up to Diane Rea in 1999
(Top) Dressed as the Doctor, Colin buries a time capsule with Lisa Jenkins in 1985

HEAR THIS: Colin Baker and Nicola Bryant promote a series of audio Doctor Who episodes in 1985

SLIPBACK

Doctor hits the airwaves after TV series is suspended

Doctor Who was dealt a cruel blow in 1985 when BBC1 controller Michael Grade axed the series.

There was such a public outcry against the move that the BBC instead agreed to suspend production on the new television series for a few months.

To cover for the lack of new episodes on TV, the series' script editor Eric Saward was commissioned by BBC Radio 4 to write a new Who story, Slipback, just for audio.

The six episodes were aired between July 25 and August 8 1985, being transmitted as part of a children's magazine show called Pirate Radio Four.

To promote the show, stars Colin Baker and Nicola Bryant – with an impressive ghetto blaster – took to the streets to spread the word.

THE MYSTERIOUS PLANET

When Doctor Who returned from its 18-month hiatus, the Mirror was there to capture the moment when shooting resumed.

Colin Baker was back as the Doctor for its 23rd season, and Nicola Bryant returned for two more stories, before leaving the TARDIS.

The new season had an over-arching storyline, The Trial of a Time Lord, which was composed of four shorter adventures.

The first of these was The Mysterious Planet, and was recorded at the Butser Ancient Farm Project in Butser Hill, Hampshire, which doubled for the planet Ravalox – later revealed to be Earth millions of years in the future.

Colin and Nicola had great fun on the day, as they showed that Doctor Who was definitely back in business.

HIGH-FLYING: Colin Baker joins his new colleague Bonnie Langford on stage at the Aldwych Theatre in 1986

Terror of the Vervoids

Big changes were on the way to Doctor Who towards the end of the show's 23rd season.

Nicola Bryant departed the role of Peri after two years, and was succeeded by former child star Bonnie Langford, who played computer programmer Melanie Bush.

Bonnie had a memorable introduction to the media, at the Aldwych Theatre, London in January 1986. She was appearing as Peter Pan in the theatre, and was joined on stage by Colin Baker. The pair enjoyed some high-flying antics, making for some memorable pictures.

Mel was introduced in the third Trial of a Time Lord adventure – Terror of the Vervoids – joining Colin onboard the Hyperion III spaceship where some villainous vegetation was on the loose.

Bonnie was reintroduced to the public before her first episodes were shown on TV that autumn, posing with a bearded Colin again.

However, what very few people knew at the time was that just days beforehand, Colin had been told his contract as the Doctor was not being renewed by the BBC, after BBC1 controller Michael Grade decided that a change of Doctor was in order.

Doctor Who's 24th season was commissioned, and it was to be all change once more.

DELTA AND THE BANNERMEN

It's Hi-De-Hi to Seventh Doctor McCoy

It was lucky seventh when Sylvester McCoy took on the role of the Doctor in 1987.

He was unveiled to the public, succeeding Colin Baker in the TARDIS, and after a comedic performance in his first story, Time and the Rani, the Scotsman quickly established himself in the role and won acclaim from fans and critics alike.

When the Doctor landed the TARDIS at a holiday camp in 1950s Wales, it was a case of Hi-De-Who rather than Hi-De-Hi!

Sylvester McCoy and Bonnie Langford had a ball on location at Barry Island, for Delta and the Bannermen.

And they were joined by an impressive guest list which included Don Henderson, Stubby Kaye and Hugh Lloyd, but the name that tickled them most of all was Ken Dodd!

Doddy played the Tollmaster, who operated a toll port in space and allowed the TARDIS safe passage, but a bus full of space tourists crashed on Earth, prompting the Doctor to rescue them.

Unfortunately, the vicious alien Bannermen, led by Henderson as Gavrok, were in pursuit of the last of the Chimerons, Delta.

However, love was the answer as the Bannermen were beaten, and Delta left with a new partner to repopulate her planet.

DRAGONFIRE

When the Seventh Doctor's new companion Ace was revealed to the public, she was a character with a difference.

Unlike her immediate predecessor, Sophie Aldred's character was not a screamer. She was truly a reflection of late 1980s Britain. Ace was a teenager from the streets of Perivale, coming from a single-parent family, and didn't get on with her mum.

Having left drama school, Sophie was working in theatre in Manchester when she was told by her agent that she had won the coveted role of the new assistant to Sylvester McCoy.

Sophie was unveiled to the public at a press conference by producer John Nathan-Turner, and she admitted it all came as a pleasant shock to her.

She said: "I remember the costume designer for Dragonfire, Richard Croft, took me out to buy a costume for Ace, and John also said to get me a nice outfit for the photocall.

"We ended up going to a shop just off Oxford Street, in St Christopher's Place.

"Richard was absolutely brilliant, because I was just so ungirly. I was a tomboy – I didn't wear a lot of dresses. So we ended up in this little shop, where we picked up the skirt and top, which I really liked. I was really lucky because

Ace enjoys the attention as the Seventh Doctor gets a new companion

Richard had an eye for clothing, and I didn't! I just wore what I liked.

"Actually, I've still got that skirt now. It reminds me of Richard and the excitement of those early days.

"Before we did the press call, I had no idea what to expect. I just went along to Television Centre and they stuck me in the make-up chair – it was such a luxury to be pampered and preened, and a bit of a shock for a tomboy like me!

"The props guys set up the TARDIS and I went out there with Sylvester, and we stood there and got our pictures taken. It was pretty amazing for my first appearance with what you'd now call the paparazzi.

"There were people calling my name from every direction, trying to get me to look at them, and I've got to admit, I absolutely loved it! That was just amazing, as I hadn't expected that.

"I remember John Nathan-Turner was there, puffing on his cigarette at the side, encouraging me to be a bit more sexy, but I wasn't having any of that. I did enjoy it – I'm such a poser!"

ALL DRESSED UP: Sophie Aldred with K9 in 1987 and (inset) as she was unveiled to the press in her new clothes with Sylvester McCoy

Silver Nemesis

In 1988, Doctor Who reached its silver anniversary, and to mark the occasion, the Doctor faced his silver-coloured foes – the Cybermen.

Unlike the 50th anniversary, which the BBC are promoting with full pomp and pride, celebrations for the 25th year of the show went almost under the radar with the Corporation failing to promote the show.

Instead, it was left to producer John Nathan-Turner and his stars, Sylvester McCoy and Sophie Aldred, to highlight the show's incredible achievement.

On location at Arundel Castle, which stood in for Windsor Castle, the Cybermen, the Doctor and his companion put on a memorable show for the cameras.

Sophie recalled: "We all took a break from the recording to do the photoshoot.

"All the Cybermen had to be put back into their gear, but we had this on-going problem with them at the time, because the suits that they wore were very stiff and the paint they put on them to make them silver was reacting with the material. They got this thing that we called Cyber-crotch, because they kept splitting there!

"The poor old designers were all going round with gaffer tape, to put it on the right bits.

"Sylvester and I were really happy to play along for the cameras with a birthday cake.

"We also did a few pictures with an actress who looked like the Queen in front of the castle. It was always good fun doing those shoots with Sylvester."

As well as the publicity shoot on location during the recording of Silver Nemesis, Sylvester and Sophie later did another event to mark the show's 25th birthday in London.

Sophie added: "We did that one at the Space Centre, and they were great.

"Sadly, the BBC weren't that bothered, but the Space Centre went to so much trouble, getting a TARDIS cake – it was great."

SILVER CELEBRATIONS: Sylvester McCoy and Sophie Aldred marked the show's landmark on location at Arundel Castle and at the Space Centre (top)

BATTLEFIELD

Legends return for four-episode Arthurian special as resurgent show recorded final series of the 20th century

Doctor Who was on its last legs in 1989, as the BBC's support for the series waned.

For years, it had been allowed to stagger on with no love shown by the BBC's management, and was allowed to die a quiet death.

But ironically, the show had been turned around by imaginative and clever scripts which had been commissioned by script editor Andrew Cartmel, and was in better health in 1989 than it had been in years.

The first story to be recorded in that 26th and final 20th century series was Battlefield, which guest starred former companion Jean Marsh as evil witch Morgaine, and also marked the return of Nicholas Courtney as Brigadier Alistair Lethbridge-Stewart.

The story was based on the legend of Arthur, as knights from another dimension sought to reclaim Excalibur.

The cast were joined on location by the Daily Mirror, who were there to record the four episodes at Rutland Water in Leicestershire.

And while Sophie Aldred was back for her second full season as Ace, she was delighted with another guest star in the story – the Third Doctor's old yellow car, Bessie!

Sophie said: "For me, that was just brilliant – I had the chance to see Bessie again. She was stuck in my mind as part of my childhood, as I'd grown up with Doctor Who in the seventies. Jon Pertwee was my original Doctor.

"It was a real honour to be allowed to clamber all over her for that photoshoot.

"We had a wonderful location in Rutland

Water, which lent itself very well to the shoot, as it was just so green and pleasant.

"I remember having a real laugh and an amazing time, meeting people like Jean Marsh, and the wonderful Nicholas Courtney as the Brigadier, who was a real legend in Doctor Who, and another part of my childhood."

BESSIE RIDES AGAIN: The Third Doctor's yellow car, Jean Marsh and Nicholas Courtney all returned to appear in Battlefield

THE FOURTH DIMENSION: *A quartet of Doctors pose with the Dalek Supreme in 1993*

I n 1993, Doctor Who commemorated its 30th anniversary.

Like its 25th birthday, there wasn't too much in the way of a major celebration from the BBC.

But it didn't stop four incarnations of the Time Lord from gathering at the Hammersmith Ark, to promote the opening of an exhibition to mark the occasion.

Third Doctor Jon Pertwee joined his fifth, sixth and seventh incarnations, Peter Davison, Colin Baker and Sylvester McCoy, at the event on April 27 1993.

The four encountered an old foe, when they met the Dalek Supreme at the venue, and also had the chance to try out some brick-like mobile phones – a far cry from the sonic screwdriver!

The quartet had hoped to be working together when the BBC announced they would be producing The Dark Dimension, an anniversary special which was initially planned as a straight-to-video special release, starring Jon,

The 30th aniversary

Peter, Colin and Sylvester, as well as Fourth Doctor Tom Baker.

Shortly after announcing The Dark Dimension, which was later planned to be shown on television, the BBC announced the feature-length episode was being scrapped. It later emerged that a miscalculation of £250,000 would have resulted in the whole project, including estimated video sales, running at a break-even figure, rather than making a profit for the BBC.

THE TV MOVIE

A short but successful spell as McGann takes Doctor to Canada

For one glorious night, Doctor Who returned to our screens in 1996.

A multi-million pound TV movie was produced in Canada, after executive producer Philip Segal, an ex-pat Brit, obtained the rights to make the show.

Segal, who had worked for Steven Spielberg's Amblin Pictures when negotiations were ongoing, was a long-term fan of the series, having watched it on his grandfather's knee before his family emigrated to the States.

Many high-profile names were linked with the part over the years, including Donald Sutherland, Sylvester Stallone and Eric Idle, but the part was eventually won by Paul McGann – who beat his brother Mark to the part!

Sylvester McCoy joined the party too, as his old enemy the Master caused the TARDIS to crashland in San Francisco on New Year's Eve in 1999, and caused mayhem as the new millennium celebrations were about to get underway.

After being accidentally shot by a street gang, the Doctor was taken to hospital where he was treated by Dr Grace Holloway, whose anaesthetic accidentally killed the Doctor's alien physiognomy. In the hospital morgue, the Doctor regenerated into the dashing McGann.

The TV movie was a huge ratings success in Britain, gaining 9.1 million views on May 27 1996, but unfortunately it was scheduled against the final episode of Roseanne in America, gaining 5.6 million views.

This wasn't enough to convince the American TV networks to commission a new series on the back of the TV Movie, and the Eighth Doctor appeared to be dead in the water.

However, in 2001, London-based Big Finish Productions began producing new audio adventures starring McGann, licensed by the BBC. As well as battling Daleks, Cybermen and Zygons, he was joined by India Fisher, best known as the narrator of Masterchef, as Edwardian adventuress Charlotte 'Charley' Pollard, and later Two Pints of Lager and a Packet of Crisps star Sheridan Smith, as Lucie Miller.

Although he may only have been the Doctor for just over an hour on TV in 1996, McGann has a legion of fans, who live in hope that he will return to play the Doctor once more, even if it is only to see him briefly regenerate into his successor.

DASHING: Paul McGann's time as the Doctor was brief, but many fans would like to see him take the role again one day

"The TV movie was a huge ratings success, gaining 9.1 million views"

ROSE

The news Doctor Who fans had been waiting for...

In 2003, with Doctor Who having been off air since the TV Movie starring Paul McGann as the Doctor, the show's fans were given the perfect 40th anniversary present.

The BBC revealed that a new series of Doctor Who had been commissioned, would be produced in Wales, and the man in charge of production was Russell T Davies.

The Welshman was well-known in television circles as a Doctor Who fan, and his credentials were there for all to see. Best known for his ground-breaking series Queer as Folk, one of his lead characters had been a Doctor Who fan, and K9 had featured in an episode. Davies had also written an original Doctor Who novel featuring Seventh Doctor Sylvester McCoy in 1996, Damaged Goods.

Over the course of the next few months, Davies began to assemble his production team, ready for shooting to begin in July 2004. His biggest task, though, was finding actors to take on the roles of the Doctor and his new companion.

Speculation ranged from the sublime to the ridiculous, before it was finally revealed that the Ninth Doctor would be Christopher Eccleston. The former Cracker star had made his name playing intense roles, and got in touch with Davies to put his name forward for the Doctor. The pair had previously worked together on ITV drama The Second Coming.

Casting the Doctor's new companion was a difficult task, as she was to be the eyes of a new generation of viewers, introducing them to the fantastical world of the Time Lord, his TARDIS, and their travels into the past and the future, as well as alien worlds.

The part went to former pop star Billie Piper, and she very quickly won over viewers and critics as Rose Tyler, a down-on-her-luck shopworker, who stumbled into the Doctor's life during an encounter with his old foes the Autons – shop dummies made from plastic, controlled by the Nestene Intelligence, last seen battling Third Doctor Jon Pertwee.

When shooting on Doctor Who began, the Mirror was there to capture moves from the first episode of the new series, Rose, as the TARDIS was erected on the streets of Cardiff, and watched as Billie Piper ran out of the department store.

The new take on Doctor Who was an overnight success, and although Eccleston may only have played the Doctor in 13 episodes, his contribution to relaunching Doctor Who in the 21st century cannot be overlooked.

BOOM TOWN

The TARDIS goes on a Welsh tour as excitment builds towards launch of the first Doctor Who series of the 21st century

As shooting on the first series of Doctor Who in the 21st century came to a close, interest was running high before it went on air.

Teaser trailers started appearing on television, before its big launch at Easter 2005.

Very quickly, the public fell in love with the Doctor and Rose – who were later joined on their travels by John Barrowman as Captain Jack Harkness.

The series required a nine month-long shoot to get all 13 episodes recorded, with the TARDIS becoming a regular sight in and around the streets of Wales.

In early February 2005, the TARDIS landed in Roald Dahl Plass, showcasing the magnificent Cardiff Bay area, which had been redeveloped over the years.

The episode Boom Town was unlike other episodes in the series as it featured the Welsh capital as itself, rather than doubling up for anywhere else.

Christopher Eccleston, Billie Piper and John Barrowman were joined on location by Noel Clarke, who played Mickey Smith, Rose's boyfriend who she dumped to join the Doctor on his travels.

The quartet joined forces to defeat the villainous Margaret Slitheen (or by Blon Fel-Fotch Passameer-Day Slitheen to give her her proper name), from the planet Raxacoricofallapatorius, who planned to destroy Cardiff and the Earth.

Soon after the first episode of the series was broadcast, it was announced that Christopher Eccleston had chosen to leave the series, but the Tenth Doctor was already waiting in the wings.

WELSH WONDER: The Doctor Who cast on location in Cardiff Bay

TOOTH AND CLAW

When David Tennant became the Doctor in 2005, it fulfilled the young actor's dream.

The Scotsman, who was 33 at the time, had previously played guest roles in various Doctor Who audio plays from Big Finish Productions, opposite his predecessors Colin Baker and Sylvester McCoy – and was over the moon to succeed Christopher Eccleston in the TARDIS.

When it came to casting a new Doctor, executive producer Russell T Davies looked to his leading man from another show which he had just made for the BBC, Casanova.

Russell said: "When I first saw the audition tape for Casanova, I didn't know who he was. I wasn't looking for a big star, and this was before Blackpool had been on, but I knew he was a well-known talent in Scotland.

"We saw him, we loved him and we cast him and enjoyed working with him.

"I also knew he was a big Doctor Who fan!

"Although Casanova was nothing to do with Doctor Who, as it was a separate production made by a separate company, when we learned Chris was leaving it all just fitted together very nicely.

"We didn't screentest him, having just done

three hours of Casanova with David, and by that time I'd seen Blackpool."

And David recalled: "I remember being thrilled to bits when I got asked, and then thinking, 'Is this a good idea?' It didn't last long!"

However, there was controversy soon after David was cast, when it was revealed he wouldn't be using his natural accent.

Russell explained: "I didn't ban the accent – it was just part of the creation of David's Doctor. We talked about the costume, as, for example, we didn't say David would have to wear the suit. It was just a cast of human beings coming together and talking about things."

David said: "When Russell came to me, that was how he asked me to play it. I wouldn't say I was disappointed, it's just what I was asked to do.

"I've always known that part of working as an actor was to take on different accents.

"It doesn't make me any less Scottish because I'm not using my Scottish accent.

"It didn't bother me, but it was nice to get the chance to do one episode where the Doctor came up with the idea of slipping into a Scottish accent which, remarkably, the Doctor can do!"

David's co-star Billie Piper added: "In the Christmas episode, the idea was that Rose's

accent would have rubbed off on the Doctor, but we never actually got around to filming it."

David said: "It was like a chick imprinting on someone when it comes out of an egg."

Comparing the two Doctors, Billie said of David and Chris: "They are different people and bring different things. David's Doctor is a lot more emotional, while Chris' Doctor was more intense.

"Of course they are going to have a different approach, but they are playing the same part. A new person rubs off on you very quickly, and you adjust – she moved with the times and the man."

David didn't get the chance to meet his predecessor at the regeneration, as it was shot weeks apart.

He said: "I didn't unfortunately, because of the way it had to be shot – we shot the regeneration on separate days. We haven't bumped into each other, unfortunately. I'm sure we will at some point."

David's third story as the Doctor, Tooth and Claw, saw the TARDIS land in Scotland, which delighted the actor.

He said: "It wasn't a specific ambition, but story-wise, it's nice if you move the characters around and take them to different places. Obviously with filming in Wales, Cardiff has had a shout.

"I was quite keen that Scotland should get a shout and it has certain personal ramifications as well. We filmed in Wales, but there's one shot where on the hillside, they've added a little bit of purple heather. But on the whole, it's remarkably similar with some of the landscape we have up here, so there wasn't a lot that needed doing."

Tooth and Claw was a dark story, featuring grisly deaths, but David denied that the series was too scary.

He said of Tooth and Claw: "I think it does push it quite far, but it's still, ultimately, very responsibly done. It's within a fantastic environment and children understand that too.

"I think that's part of growing up, being scared. That's what Doctor Who has done since 1963 and I'm glad to see it continuing to do so.

"A gore-fest would be ridiculous – there's no blood, and it was just fun.

"I think Doctor Who has had horror elements for as long as I can remember. It tours the genres - in the first one we were in a hospital five billion years in the future, then we were in Scotland and it's gothic horror, the next week is a kind of Grange Hill. It's what Doctor Who does best – every week it's a new style of story."

SCOT THE LOT: The cast enjoy shooting Tooth and Claw on location in Wales

THE IDIOT'S LANTERN

The Doctor and his companion build a closer bond as Tennant reveals pitfalls of taking on such an important acting role

There was a touch of 50s glamour when the TARDIS brought the Doctor and Rose to London in David Tennant's second season.

In The Idiot's Lantern, Billie Piper donned a stunning period costume, while David had his hair made into a quiff, as they drove on a Vespa scooter, to defeat the face-stealing Wire on the eve of the Queen's coronation.

As with many 21st century Doctor Who stories, although the episode was set in London, it was mostly recorded in Cardiff.

And there was an amusing in-joke for TV fans as writer Mark Gatiss set the action in Florizel Street – the working title for Coronation Street!

David's first full series saw the Doctor and Rose growing closer than ever before, building on the friendship which was established with the Ninth Doctor.

"The Doctor and companion has always been very important," said David, "particularly in this series, but the way Russell writes it, it's always an emotional thing, which maybe the show hadn't had before. Rose's family ultimately became the Doctor's family.

"In episode eight, it looks like we're cut off from everything, forever, and we have a quiet moment to consider that idea of never returning home."

David admitted that putting himself in the spotlight as Doctor Who would mean his every action was analysed by the series' devoted fans, for years to come, as well as putting himself in the firing line for TV critics.

He said: "I don't think anybody ever likes being told they are not good at what they do. You invest a lot into what you do. You want everyone to tell you you are great all the time, but I'm wise enough to know what to expect.

"A show like this receives so much scrutiny and analysis, you are never going to please all the people, all the time."

BACK TO THE FIFTIES: David Tennant and Billie Piper in period costume while filming The Idiot's Lantern

The Last of the Time Lords

David Tennant's second year as the Doctor ended with a bang.

With Billie Piper having departed as Rose, he was joined on his travels by Martha Jones, played by Freema Agyeman, and during a brief stop-off for the TARDIS to refuel in Cardiff, at a space-time rift, the pair were joined by Captain Jack Harkness, with John Barrowman returning to the show.

Since leaving the Doctor and Rose during Christopher Eccleston's final adventure, Captain Jack had returned to Earth, basing himself with the Cardiff-centred Torchwood organisation.

After Doctor Who's success, showrunner Russell T Davies was asked to create a spinoff series for BBC, which became known as Torchwood – an anagram of Doctor Who – that saw Jack and his friends Gwen Cooper, Ianto Jones, Dr Owen Harper and Toshiko Sato investigating alien activities centred around a space-time rift in Cardiff.

At the end of Torchwood's first series, Jack heard the TARDIS materialise and ran for the police box.

The ship travelled to the far future, where the Doctor and his friends met the last human beings, searching for a new world to live on. They were assisted by Professor Yana – really the Doctor's old enemy the Master, suffering from amnesia.

After defeating the Master's plan to rule the Earth, Jack wanted to return to Earth to be with his Torchwood friends, and he was left at the entrance to his secret headquarters, located in Cardiff's Roald Dahl Plass. Pictured here are the crew recording the end of the story.

Barrowman particularly enjoyed working with fellow Scot David Tennant, with the pair quickly becoming firm friends – although Freema would complain that the boys would regularly have farting competitions inside the TARDIS police box prop!

HUNGRY FOR SUCCESS: Matt Smith emerged as the new Doctor and quickly made the part his own

THE HUNGRY EARTH

When David Tennant announced he was leaving the TARDIS in the autumn of 2008, it came as a real surprise to everyone.

It was even more of a surprise when it was announced that Steven Moffat, who had succeeded Russell T Davies as the Doctor Who showrunner, had picked a virtually unknown 26-year-old as the next Doctor.

But very quickly it became apparent that what Matt Smith may have lacked in years, he more than made up for in talent.

With his amazingly flopping fringe, his bow tie and tweed jacket, combined with a swagger of a drunk giraffe, Matt very quickly made the part his own.

The new Doctor went on location for two-part story The Hungry Earth/Cold Blood, in October 2009, as he recorded his first season.

In the story, a drilling operation disturbs a colony of Silurians, the reptilian species that inhabited the Earth before mankind emerged.

Scots actress Karen Gillan had been cast as his assistant Amy Pond, and they were later joined in their adventures by Arthur Darvill as Amy's boyfriend Rory.

Guest starring was Goodness Gracious Me's Meera Syal as scientist Nasreen Chaudhry.

The shoot took place at Bedwellty Pits, Tredegar, just outside Cardiff.

THE DOCTOR, THE WIDOW AND THE WARDROBE

The Doctor Who Christmas special is a highlight of the festive season each year, and 2011 was no different.

The Doctor, The Widow and the Wardrobe saw the Eleventh Doctor turn up to save Christmas for the Arwell family, who were grieving after their loss of father Reg, in World War II.

Before the story proper began, the Doctor had to stop some aggressive aliens, and blew up their spaceship high above the Earth.

Unfortunately, he was thrown out into space – but was able to salvage an abandoned space suit and put it on before he was killed.

The Doctor crashlanded in Britain, during the war years, and made his way to a nearby police box – mistaking it for the TARDIS!

This scene was recorded in Y Groes, Rhiwbina, Cardiff, on September 26 2011.

MIRROR MAN

Matt Smith's Mirror appearance pleases his grandad

The Daily Mirror was given the Doctor's official seal of approval in March 2010!

The Eleventh Doctor, Matt Smith, was joined by Karen Gillan on a visit to our headquarters at Canary Wharf, to see what goes into the production of the intelligent tabloid.

They were given a guided tour of our offices, and shown around the different departments, to learn how the paper is put together.

And Matt jokingly offered to 'tweak' some of our hi-tech equipment with his sonic screwdriver.

He admitted his family are big Mirror fans, especially his grandad.

Matt said: "He gets the paper every day and always has done. He'll be really delighted to see me in it."

And flame-haired Karen added: "Matt's eccentric, endearing – and funny without even knowing it."

INSPECT THE GADGET: *Matt Smith shows off his sonic screwdriver on a visit to the Mirror offices*

MATT SMITH

FANS' FAVOURITE:
Karen Gillan meets
Doctor Who fans
in Glasgow, where
new action figures
were on sale

Karen Gillan comes home

On Saturday, August 28, 2010, Doctor Who fans in Scotland were given a real treat.

Karen Gillan returned to her homeland, giving the Doctor Who faithful a rare chance to meet one of the stars of the show on her home soil, without having to travel to a convention in England.

Karen visited Hamleys flagship store in Glasgow, in the St Enoch Shopping Centre, for her first in-store signing event.

Since Doctor Who's return to television, there was a plethora of officially licensed merchandise available for fans to buy. The most popular of these were action figures, produced by Character Options – and commissioned by Karen's fellow Scot Alasdair Dewar.

Karen was immortalised in plastic, and she was delighted to be able to officially launch the Amy Pond action figure.

Speaking before her visit, Karen enthused: "I'm so excited to be travelling up to Scotland to introduce Doctor Who fans to my new Amy Pond action figure. I can't wait to meet everyone."

In order to meet Karen and get an autograph, fans gathered for Hamleys doors' opening at 9am in order to obtain a wristband, with just 200 fans given the chance to meet her.

People were queuing from 6am that day, travelling from all over Scotland and the north of England to try to get the chance to meet their idol.

And although there was a lengthy queue before Karen arrived, spirits were high in the crowd as young and old fans alike waited to meet Karen.

And afterwards, everyone who had stood for hours agreed it had been well worth their while.

MEET CLARA OSWALD

Doctor Who team breaks with tradition by introducing Jenna Louise to the world

On March 21 2012, the Doctor Who production team did something that hadn't previously been done on the show since 1987 – they held a photocall to introduce the new companion.

When it was announced that Karen Gillan would be leaving Doctor Who, speculation was rife about who would be her replacement.

It was finally announced by the show's executive producer Steven Moffat that the former Emmerdale and Waterloo Road actress Jenna Louise Coleman would be the new TARDIS traveller alongside Matt Smith.

Steven told the Mirror: "We saw a lot of brilliant actresses, but Jenna was the only person going faster than Matt – he had to keep up!"

Blackpool-born Jenna said she was "a huge fan" of the show and wanted "to get started already.

"Matt Smith did my audition with me. It was fun and I felt like we were in it together."

Jenna first came to the public's attention in ITV soap Emmerdale, in which she played teenager Jasmine Thomas. She landed the part in 2005, while she was still auditioning for drama schools and lived in a shared flat.

In 2007 Jenna was nominated for Best Newcomer at the British Soap Awards and Most Popular Newcomer at the National Television Awards. Two years later she had more industry nominations under her belt, including Best Actress and Sexiest Female at the Soap Awards and had also won a part in the BBC's Waterloo Road as tough school girl Lindsay James.

Although she was cast in March, it was announced that her first appearance as the new companion would be in 2012 Christmas special The Snowmen – but fans were stunned to see her appear in the first episode of the 2012 series Asylum of the Daleks, as spaceship survivor Oswin Oswald.

However, at the end of the adventure, it was revealed she was really a Dalek – and died!

The Doctor later encountered Clara Oswald, as played by Jenna Louise, in both Victorian London, where she died again, and in the present day, where he was keen to solve the mystery of the impossible girl.

PICTURE PERFECT:
Jenna Louise Coleman
faces the press
after joining the
Doctor Who cast